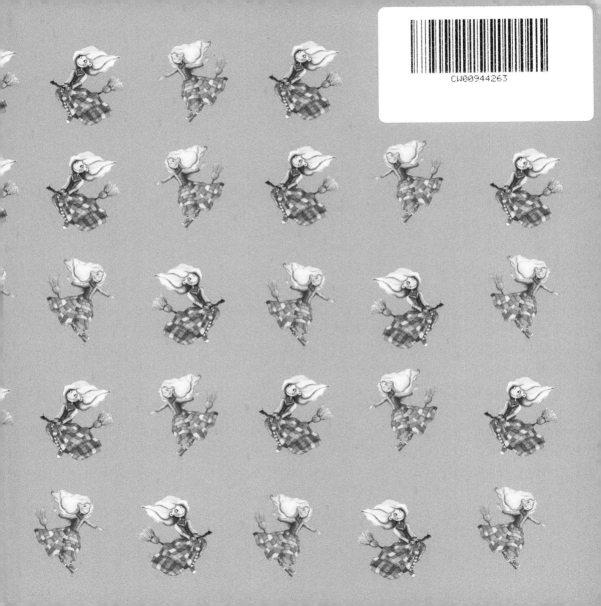

Libby Edwards
Illustrations by Catherine Jackman

Trixibelle and the Birthday Spell

Bumblebee Books
London

BUMBLEBEE PAPERBACK EDITION

Copyright © Libby Edwards 2021
Illustrations by Catherine Jackman

A CIP catalogue record for this title is
available from the British Library.

ISBN: 978-1-83934-182-3

Bumblebee Books is an imprint of
Olympia Publishers.

First Published in 2021

Bumblebee Books
Tallis House
2 Tallis Street
London
EC4Y 0AB

Printed in Great Britain

www.olympiapublishers.com

Dedication

For Tony Bailey-Hughes,
who loved the magic of children's books.

Trixibelle, Trixibelle
the wonderful witch,
who makes things well
with a wave of her wand
and a magical spell
the wonderful witch that is Trixibelle.

With Boris the butler
and Doris the cat
her dancing broom
and her pointy hat
with a wave of her wand
and a magical spell...

the wonderful
world of
Trixibelle.

It was nine o'clock on a Friday morning when Trixibelle the Witch arrived home in a puff of smoke. This was no ordinary Friday. Today was Trixibelle's birthday! She had planned a party and was feeling very excited.

Trixibelle wondered how many of her friends had replied to her party invitation. She asked Boris the butler to bring her the post. The post was piled up high.

Trixibelle sat down in her higgledy piggledy kitchen with Doris, her purple cat. Boris made Trixibelle a nice cup of tea as she read her letters.

Humpty Dumpty, Little Miss Muffet and the three little pigs could all come to her birthday party! Trixibelle was very pleased.

The party was that afternoon, but Trixibelle had only just remembered that she needed a party dress. She looked in her wardrobe, but all of her dresses were old and tatty. Trixibelle decided that she needed a brand-new dress.

Trixibelle took her 'Stitches for Witches' dress-making book off the shelf and sat down in her higgledy piggledy kitchen to begin sewing. She couldn't thread the needle or cut the material in a straight line. Trixibelle was in such a pickle!

Doris suggested that it was time for a

spell.

Boris gave Trixibelle her spell book. She polished her magic wand and flicked to the dress-making spell.
The three ingredients were:
Silk thread
Cobweb thread
A handful of stardust (for added sparkle)

Oh dear! Trixibelle didn't have any of these things!

There was only one thing for it! Trixibelle snapped her fingers and her broomstick danced out of the broom cupboard.

It danced all the way to the kitchen window, tapped three times on the glass, and the window flew open with a gust of wind. Boris and Doris waved goodbye to Trixibelle as she hopped onto her broomstick.

Trixibelle flew high up into the sky over towns and mountains until she spotted the glowing treetops of the magical forest.

She could hear the fairies and pixies playing amongst the bluebells.

Trixibelle landed very carefully next to a giant toadstool.

Just as Trixibelle stepped off her broomstick, she spotted a white cocoon lying on a leaf. It was Sally the silkworm sleeping in the sun.

Trixibelle woke her up gently and asked, "Please can I have some silk for my dress-making spell? It's my birthday you see and I need a new party dress."

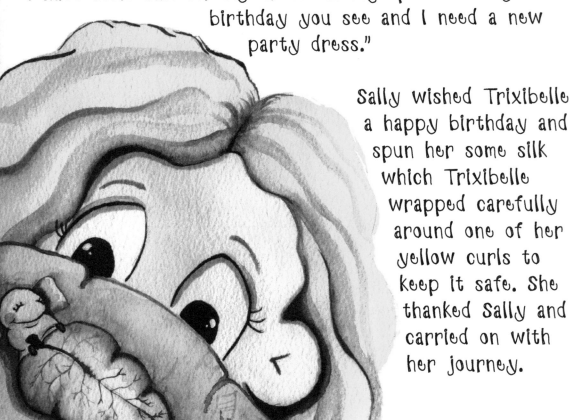

Sally wished Trixibelle a happy birthday and spun her some silk which Trixibelle wrapped carefully around one of her yellow curls to keep it safe. She thanked Sally and carried on with her journey.

Just then, Trixibelle
spotted Miss Muffet who,
as always, was sat on a tuffet.
Just the person, thought
Trixibelle. She told Miss Muffet that she needed some
cobweb thread to help her with a dress-making spell.
The spider who was sat beside Miss Muffet, hopped onto
Trixibelle's head and spun a web in her curls. Trixibelle
thanked the spider, who scurried off in a hurry.

Miss Muffet
wished Trixibelle
a happy birthday
and said that
she would see
her later at
the party.

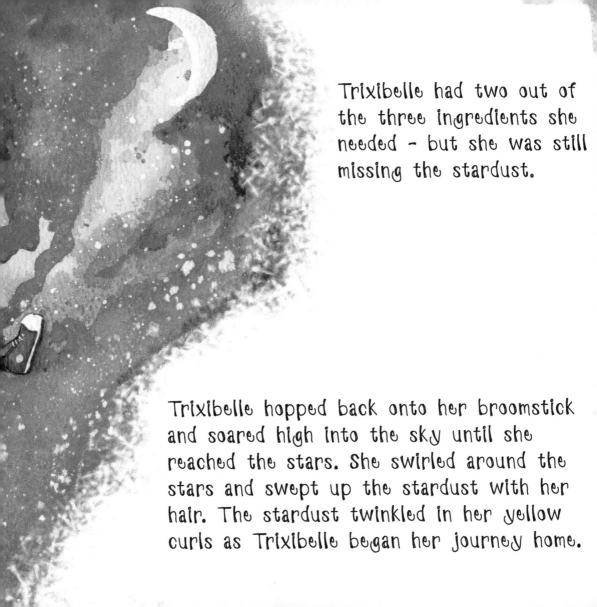

Trixibelle had two out of the three ingredients she needed - but she was still missing the stardust.

Trixibelle hopped back onto her broomstick and soared high into the sky until she reached the stars. She swirled around the stars and swept up the stardust with her hair. The stardust twinkled in her yellow curls as Trixibelle began her journey home.

Back in the higgledy piggledy kitchen, Boris and Doris waited for Trixibelle to come home.

Suddenly there was a loud wooosh as the kitchen window flew open and Trixibelle landed on the table. Her red boots thudded on the wood.

She snapped her fingers and her broomstick danced back into the broom cupboard.

Trixibelle unwound the silk thread from her curl, plucked out the cobweb and shook her hair until all the stardust had sprinkled onto the table. She showed the ingredients to Boris and Doris, picked up her wand and read out the dress-making spell from her spellbook.....

"Spin the silk and wiggle your nose, thread the web and wiggle your toes, a sprinkle of stars and a one two three, make a party dress just for me!"

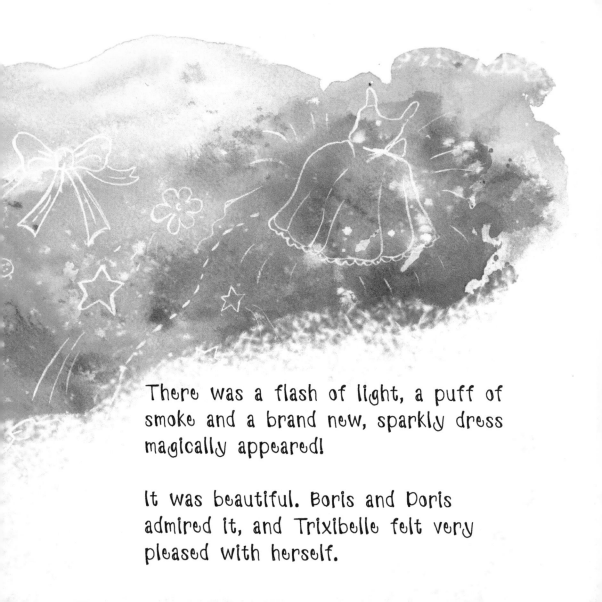

There was a flash of light, a puff of smoke and a brand new, sparkly dress magically appeared!

It was beautiful. Boris and Doris admired it, and Trixibelle felt very pleased with herself.

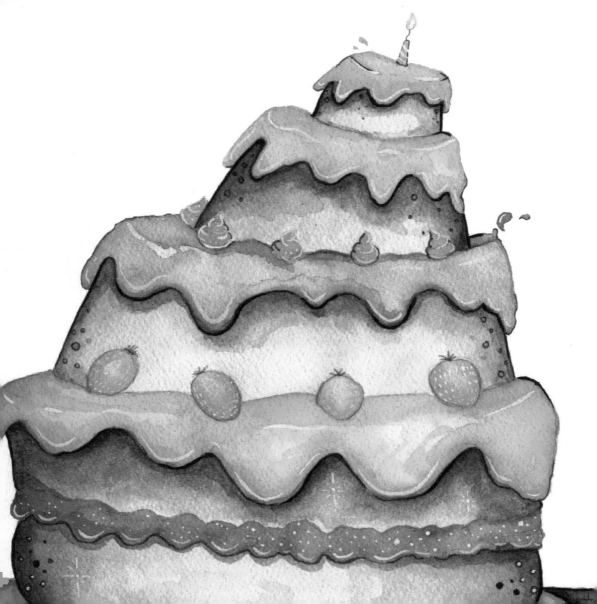

Trixibelle went upstairs to change into her new dress. When she returned, she saw a huge pink birthday cake on the kitchen table. While Trixibelle had been away, Boris and Doris had baked her a cake! They had also prepared some delicious snacks for the party. Crunchy crabapple creams, juicy jam jellyroll and wiggly watermelon waffles. Yummy! Just then, the doorbell rang...

All of Trixibelle's friends had arrived in time for the party! Trixibelle thought what a wonderful birthday it was.

She had a beautiful new dress, a delicious cake and lots of good friends to help her celebrate!

About the Author

Libby Edwards likes to create magical experiences for people of all ages. She writes books and theatre scripts and produces shows, workshops and events. Libby lives in North Wales and runs a Theatrical Production Company, Magic Light Productions, producing pantomimes, magic & illusions, plays and children's theatre across the UK. She brings theatre into schools through workshops which enrich the curriculum. She also produces, makes and performs with 'The Magic Light Puppets', creating dark light puppet shows and running puppet workshops. Through her children's books, Libby encourages imagination and play, needed more than ever in the current climate.

Acknowledgements

Thank you to Catherine Jackman for bringing Trixibelle and her friends to life with beautiful, enchanting illustrations, Jacqueline Downs for editing, encouraging and supporting throughout, Linda-Mary & Margaret for always being there to love and lend a hand, and to Stuart, for constant inspiration.

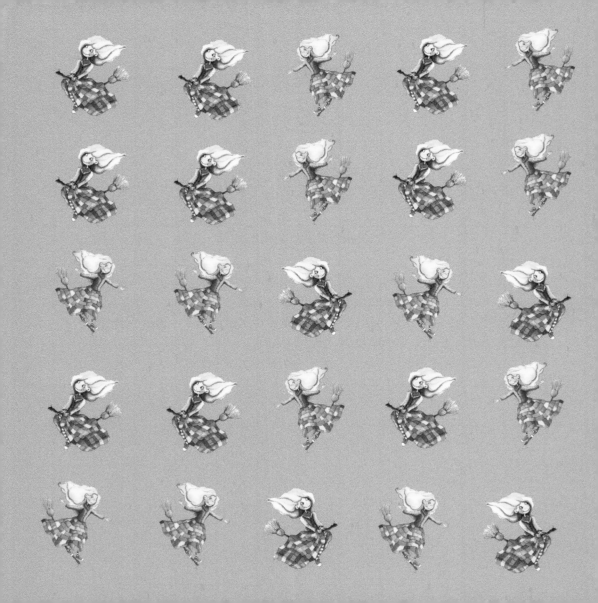